PRINCE
EDWARD'S
FEAST

Written by
Robin O'Brien

Illustrated by
Leah-Ellen Heming

meadowside
CHILDREN'S BOOKS

O nce upon a time, in a sweet distant land of milk and honey, the Queen waved goodbye to the King.

"I'm off to market," she said, "and I want that baby fed by the time I get **back!**"

Prince Edward was
the apple of his daddy's eye so the King
treated him to his favourite meal
of cherry pie with a big dollop
of vanilla ice cream.

But Edward looked at
the food and started to cry.
The King was baffled,
he didn't know
why!

"I think I'll take
you to the Court Chef,
he'll give it a try!"

"Help me Chef!" said the King.
"If I don't get the baby fed,
the Queen will go bananas!"

"Very well," said the Court Chef.
"Have some of my famous pancakes.
They are the best thing
since sliced bread!"

But Edward looked at the pancakes and started to cry. The Chef was baffled, **he didn't know why!**

"I'll take you to the Court Jester, he'll give it a **try!**"

The Court Jester was as
nutty as a **fruitcake.**
He blew raspberries while
he juggled bowls of jelly

then served them
to Prince Edward.

But Edward looked at
the jelly and started to cry.
The Jester was baffled,
he didn't know why!

"I'll take you to
the Court Egg-Layer,
she'll give it a try!"

"Well, normally I only lay in the morning," clucked Miss Henrietta Egginton-Peck, the Court Egg-Layer.

"This job pays peanuts as it is! I barely earn a crust, you know!"

But she laid an egg
fit for a **k**ing.

Edward looked at the egg
and started to cry.
Henrietta was baffled,
she didn't know why!

"I'll take you
to the Court
Magician,
he'll give it
a **try**!"

"I guess you've heard
through the grapevine
how my magical stew is
good for you!"
he said.

"Well," said the King,
whose patience was wearing
wafer thin, "all this
hocus-pocus
is not my cup of tea,
but I'll give
anything a try!"

The Court Dragon Slayer
served a giant helping
of **steak and
chips!**

Edward looked at the steak and started to cry. The Dragon Slayer was baffled, he didn't know why!

"I'll take you to the Court Guards, they'll give it a **try**!"

The King grilled his guards, but they were as useless as a chocolate kettle.

And poor little Prince Edward continued to cry.

He cried...

Eventually the King
was lost for ideas!

"Edward, we've been running around like headless chickens, will you please be a peach and **eat something?!**"

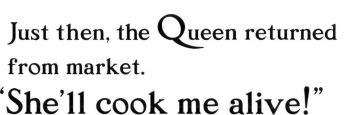

Just then, the Queen returned
from market.
"She'll cook me alive!"
said the King.

But as cool as a cucumber,
she looked at her baby and smiled.
"You really do have a memory
like a sieve my king!"

"Our little prince is missing one vital ingredient."

Can you guess what it is?

His spoon!

For Heilda Evans,
my Nan, with love

R.O'B.

For my Wonderful Uncle Anthony,
with all my love

L.E.H.

First published in 2009
by Meadowside Children's Books
185 Fleet Street, London, EC4A 2HS
www.meadowsidebooks.com

Text © Robin O'Brien
Illustrations © Leah-Ellen Heming
The rights of Robin O'Brien and Leah-Ellen Heming to be identified
as the author and illustrator of this work have been asserted by them
in accordance with the Copyright, Designs and Patents Act, 1988

A CIP catalogue record for this book is available
from the British Library

10 9 8 7 6 5 4 3 2 1

Printed in China